The Magical Myths and Lost Legends of Diwali

Priyankee Saikia is an author from Guwahati, Assam and this is her second book. She has a master's in English Literature from University of Delhi. She discovered her love for writing at the age of six, when she began penning her first few poems. Since then, she has written for a number of regional newspapers, newsletters, magazines and online blogs, besides running her college magazine. Her poetry has been published in a number of anthologies.

A former journalist, copywriter and digital marketer, Priyankee currently works as a station programming head in a leading radio company. She continues to dabble in writing during her free time and hopes to publish fiction one day. As a mother of an inquisitive five-year-old, Priyankee loves telling stories to her daughter and dreams of travelling the world with her.

In a perfect universe, the author would love nothing more than a roomful of books and all the time in the world to read them.

The Magical Myths and Lost Legends of Diwali

Priyankee Saikia

Published by
Rupa Publications India Pvt. Ltd 2021
7/16, Ansari Road, Daryaganj
New Delhi 110002

Sales centres:
Allahabad Bengaluru Chennai
Hyderabad Jaipur Kathmandu
Kolkata Mumbai

Copyright © Priyankee Saikia 2021

All rights reserved.

No part of this publication may be reproduced, transmitted, or stored in a retrieval system, in any form or by any means, electronic, mechanical, photocopying, recording or otherwise, without the prior permission of the publisher.

The views and opinions expressed in this book are the author's own and the facts are as reported by her which have been verified to the extent possible, and the publishers are not in any way liable for the same.

ISBN: 978-93-5520-142-3

First impression 2021

10 9 8 7 6 5 4 3 2 1

The moral right of the author has been asserted.

Printed at HT Media Ltd, Noida

This book is sold subject to the condition that it shall not, by way of trade or otherwise, be lent, resold, hired out, or otherwise circulated, without the publisher's prior consent, in any form of binding or cover other than that in which it is published.

To Zoe,
the brightest light of my life

Contents

Introduction   xi

Part 1
The Dawning of Diwali

1. The Origin of the Name 'Diwali'   3
2. The Happy Return of Rama after Fourteen Years in Exile   7
3. The Great Mahabharata Connection   12
4. The Oceanic Birth and the Wedding of Goddess Lakshmi   17
5. King Vikramaditya's New Calendar   22

Part 2
The Five Days of Diwali

6. Day 1: Dhanteras | How King Hima's Wife Foiled Yama's Deadly Plans   27
7. Day 2: How Krishna Freed 16,000 Princesses from the Evil King Narakasura   31

8.	Day 2: Why Hanuman Is Worshipped before Rama	36
9.	Day 3: How Goddess Kali Almost Destroyed the World	40
10.	Day 4: Govardhan Puja or Annakut | How Krishna Saved Braj Villagers by Lifting a Mountain	44
11.	Day 4: How Vishnu Tricked King Bali and Sent Him to Netherworld	48
12.	Day 5: Bhai Dooj | The Happy Reunion of Krishna and His Sister Subhadra	52

Part 3
Beyond Hindus and India

13.	The Day Lord Mahavira Attained Nirvana	59
14.	The Day Guru Hargobind Helped 52 Kings Escape from Jail	62
15.	The Day You Worship Yourself!	65
16.	Why Do Sindhis Tap Coins against Their Teeth on Diwali?	68

Part 4
Celebrations Around the Country

17.	How Odisha Observes Halloween on Diwali	73
18.	Why Is Diwali Celebrated a Month Later in Himachal Pradesh and Uttarakhand?	76
19.	Why Dogs Are Worshipped by Nepalis	80
20.	Why the Cattle Complained to Lord Shiva	83

21. Why Diwali Is Special for Newly-Weds in Tamil Nadu	87

Part 5
Other Rituals, Myths and Legends of Diwali

22. Why Did Hanuman Swallow the Sun?	93
23. The Killing of Hiranyakashipu by Narasimha	97
24. Why Are Cards Played During Diwali?	101
25. The Real Story of the Importance of Rangoli	104
26. Are Fireworks Really a Part of Diwali?	108
27. Why Are Owls Killed During Diwali?	112
Acknowledgements	115

Introduction

What is Diwali? It is so much more than just a festival of lights; it is a curious mix of a plethora of myths and legends from ancient India, which perhaps many are unaware of. These folk tales originate in the Mahabharata, the Ramayana and other such ancient scriptures; each of them playing its part in creating religious and regional traditions. Some of these traditions are still followed while observing Diwali. Most of them continue to be observed the same way since the past, while others have been modified to fit modern times. There are a few that, in my opinion, should be done away with altogether! Surprised? You will soon find out why.

This book delves deep into the origin of Diwali and what the five days of the festival entail, bringing alive each fascinating myth and legend. For instance, Lord Krishna helping rescue sixteen thousand princesses from the evil King Narakasura or Lord Hanuman bringing darkness to the entire world by swallowing the sun.

This book seeks to open the young reader's mind to the fact that Diwali is not just a Hindu festival celebrated in India. It has special meaning in different religions and in different countries too. Did you know that Diwali is observed as an official holiday in over twelve countries? Or that different animals, from dogs to crows, are worshipped in Nepal during this five-day festival? In fact, even within India, Hindus of different regions have their own twist on Diwali. While Himachal Pradesh and Uttarakhand observe Diwali a month after the rest of the country, West Bengal, unlike the rest of India, doesn't even worship Lakshmi during this festival and worships Kali instead.

Lastly, this book explores rituals and mythologies associated with Diwali that continue to remain inexplicable even to the average urban adult. Is there a story associated with playing cards on the evening of Diwali? Is the debate about fireworks during Diwali really important? Every fascinating detail around Diwali that informs, educates and delights young readers finds a place in this book. After all, what better way to understand a country than through one of its most popular festivals?

Part 1

The Dawning of Diwali

ONE

The Origin of the Name 'Diwali'

*What do you call the festival of lights:
Diwali or Deepawali/Deepavali? Well, both are right!
However, the name 'Diwali' is slightly more recent than
'Deepawali'. How is it so, do you ask?*

DEEPAVALI

The word 'Diwali' has its origin in the Sanskrit word 'Deepavali' ('Dipa' meaning a light or lamp that shines or glows; it also means knowledge and 'Avali' meaning a series or a continuous line). Put the two words together and what do you get? Yes, a row of lamps! And isn't that what Deepawali is? A festival where we traditionally light a row of earthen lamps outside our homes. Although we put up strings of colourful fairy lights in different designs and candles too. However, lighting a row of glowing earthen lamps at the threshold of the house is how this festival was celebrated several years ago.

Over time, 'Deepawali' or 'Deepavali' was shortened to 'Diwali'. But that is not all, Diwali had other names as well! One festival and so many names? Well, let us find out!

DIPAPRATIPADOTSAVA

Around 1,400 years ago, there lived a brave king called Harshavardhana (or Harsha). He used to rule over a large part of north and north-east India. He was not just a powerful emperor, but also a great writer. Historians say that he wrote not one, not two, but three Sanskrit plays! One of these plays was *Nagananda*, in which Diwali was called by a much longer name, Dipapratipadotsava. Quite a mouthful, isn't it?

> **Sshhh... Secret Author?**
> King Harsha allegedly paid his court poet, Bana, to write the plays for him.

Well, let us break down the word 'Dipapratipadotsava' in three parts to make it simpler to understand: 'Dipa', 'Pratipada' and 'Utsava'. 'Dipa' means light, 'Pratipada' means first day and 'Utsava' means festival. Put together, it literally means the festival of lights—the one that is celebrated on the first night of the Kartik month.

DIPAMALIKA

Another old name, though more recent than the version of King Harsha's rein, is Dipamalika, which found a mention in a Sanskrit play called *Kavyamimamsa* by Rajashekhara, a very famous poet. The play was written 1,100 years ago, and yet we find mention of how houses were whitewashed and decorated with pretty oil lamps during Dipamalika.

DIPOTSAVA

The different names of Diwali have been found in Indian history and not just in literature. They find a mention in ancient inscriptions of stone and copper also. But can you guess what is common between both sources? They were all in Sanskrit. A 1,000-year-old copper plate also mentions Dipotsava. It belonged to the powerful warrior king, Krsna III of the Rashtrakuta empire. By now, you can probably guess what it means. Dip (light) + Utsava (festival) = Dipotsava or Festival of Lights!

DIPOTSAVAM

Another name, Dipotsavam, finds mention in the temple inscription of an ancient Kerala king Ravivarman. Translation of the inscription reveals that this festival was celebrated by kings.

Some other interesting names include Lacshmipuja Dipanwita and Divalige. And till now, we have only been talking about the Sanskrit origin of the name!

'A rose by any other name would smell as sweet,' said William Shakespeare once, and the same is true for Diwali.

TWO

The Happy Return of Rama after Fourteen Years in Exile

The most popular legend of Diwali dates back to almost a thousand years and is connected to one of the biggest Hindu epics, the Ramayana. Filled with battles and friendships, failures and victories, and a whole lot of superpowers, it is nothing less than an adventure! The story goes...

Once upon a time, there was a king in Ayodhya called Dasharatha, who had three wives and four sons. Kaushalya's son was Rama, Kaikeyi had Bharat, and Sumitra had Lakshman and Shatrughna. Rama was the eldest, the most talented and endowed with the most superpowers. That is why his ageing father wanted to crown him king of Ayodhya. But it was not so simple. Jealousy reared its ugly head in the form of an evil maidservant, Manthara. She influenced Kaikeyi to do a very wicked thing—stop Rama from becoming the king!

Kaikeyi had two pending favours to ask of Dasharatha. She asked the king to send Rama away to the forest for an exile of fourteen years. Second, she expressed her desire to crown her own son, Bharat, as the rightful king of Ayodhya. Now, the emperor was an honourable man, and though it broke his heart, he knew he could not refuse Kaikeyi. Her wishes were his command, thanks to his code of honour. Dasharatha announced his decision and Rama, being very noble himself, took it sportingly.

However, victory did not come easy to Kaikeyi. First, Rama's wife Sita and his cousin Lakshmana refused to let him go on the exile without them. Second, Bharat was as honourable as his father and brothers. He agreed to rule Ayodhya only until Rama returned. As a symbol of his rightful reign, he kept Rama's slippers on the throne. Meanwhile, the fourteen years of exile that the trio set out on took them through quite a series of adventures. We will however concern ourselves with only the final year.

While they were living in the forest, Rama, Lakshmana and Sita were visited by a rakshasi (demoness) called Surpanakha, Ravana's sister. She tried to befriend Rama, and then Lakshmana, and when both refused her advances, she tried to kill Sita. In a fit of rage, Lakshmana cut off her nose and ears. And this started off a series of battles that the Ramayana is famous for. After all, Ravana was not going to take this insult to his sister lying down!

Rama and Lakshmana won once against the rakshasas, but the war was far from over. Ravana plotted with another rakshasa called Maricha, who transformed into a beautiful golden deer to entice Sita. When Sita spotted the golden deer near the hut, she asked Rama to go capture it for her. While Rama went looking for the deer Lakshmana guarded Sita.

What is taking Rama so long? Sita wondered as she waited eagerly for his return. When Sita finally heard Rama calling out her name from far, she asked Lakshmana to receive him. He left reluctantly but not before drawing a magical boundary around their hut. This would repel anyone from entering, thus protecting his sister-in-law. He also asked Sita to stay inside the boundary's protective spell and not step outside it. However, once she was alone, Ravana came disguised as a beggar. He tricked her into stepping out of the Lakshmana Rekha and then kidnapped her. He kidnapped her on his flying chariot, the Pushpak Vimana, and flew her away to his kingdom in Lanka. Jatayu, a demigod in a bird's avatar, tried to stop him, but Ravana fought him off

> **NOT JUST A BAD GUY!**
>
> In Hinduism, Ravana, with his ten heads, is a symbol of evil that must be defeated. But did you know that he was also one of the staunchest devotees of Shiva and is, in fact, worshipped in many parts of north and west India. He was also an intelligent king, his ten heads representing wisdom.

and made good their escape.

Meanwhile, Rama was following the golden deer a long distance away from their hut and had finally killed it. While dying, Maricha transformed back to his real form and called out to Lakshmana and Sita in Rama's voice. That is how he managed to confuse the two back at the hut! When Lakshmana met Rama, they both realized they had been tricked. They rushed back to the hut only to find Sita gone. Jataya gave Rama an eyewitness account of how Ravana had kidnapped Sita and dragged her to Lanka.

On their journey to Lanka, Rama and Lakshmana came across the ape citadel Kishkindha. There, the brothers helped Sugriva win the throne by defeating his brother Vali. In return, the apes agreed to help Rama on his quest. It is here that they met Hanuman, Rama's biggest devotee, for the first time. To confirm that Sita had indeed been taken to Lanka, Hanuman proceeded to Ravana's fortress capital. He grew his size manifold, towering over the seas and crossed them in one giant leap!

Hanuman had to fight many demons and demonesses in Lanka to get to Sita. However, when he finally met her, Sita refused to go with him, saying it should be her husband that defeated Ravana and not Hanuman. So, Hanuman left her with Rama's ring as a token, and promised that he would be back soon. He left Lanka but not before setting the city on fire. He killed Ravana's warriors and destroyed all he could, save for the area that Sita was held captive in.

As Rama and his army made their way to Lanka, they

saw stones with Rama's name etched on them floating in the sea. His army used these stones to construct a floating bridge called Rama Setu to reach Lanka.

Soon, Rama's soldiers fought tooth and nail against Ravana's army, but the latter was not easy to defeat. Every time Rama's arrows severed one of Ravana's heads, it would grow back, adding to his might. Well, behind every great man or woman, there is a supportive team that helps the mission along. In Rama's case, it was his charioteer Matali, on whose advice Rama finally picked up the most powerful arrow in his arsenal—the legendary Arrow of Brahma—to kill Ravana.

Vibhishana, Ravana's estranged brother, was on Rama's side. He advised Rama to shoot the arrow right at Ravana's navel, where he hid his elixir of immortality given by Shiva.

And that was how the most powerful king of Lanka was taken down. Rama was Lord Vishnu's seventh avatar, so by that accord, he was the chosen one to kill Ravana. After Rama rescued Sita, the entire army, led by Hanuman, returned to Ayodhya.

For the trio, it was a glorious return to their kingdom after fourteen long years in exile and a grand adventure. People cleaned their houses and lit diyas to welcome their beloved prince. The diyas that could be seen from afar were to guide the returning party home. And that is how the festival of Diwali began.

THREE

The Great Mahabharata Connection

The Ramayana is not the only Hindu epic to have a myth associated with the origin of Diwali. The Mahabharata too is believed to have certain associations with the origins of this festival, though the legitimacy of this detail is difficult to prove. Let us take a look.

Once upon a time, thousands of years ago, there lived a brave king called Pandu. He was the king of Hastinapur. He worked hard to make it a great kingdom. And then one day, he went away to a forest on a self-imposed exile with his two wives, Madri and Kunti. He handed over the throne to his blind brother, Dhritarashtra.

Pandu lived in the forest for many years. There, he and his wives had five sons, conceived through the divine blessings of different gods. The sons' names were Yudhishthira, Bhima,

Arjuna, Nakula and Sahadeva—together they were called the Pandavas. After Pandu and Madri died, Kunti took the five boys and returned to Hastinapur.

This homecoming was an exciting event for Dhritarashtra as he would meet his nephews for the first time. The people in the kingdom were also thrilled. After all, Pandu had been a loved king who had brought about immense prosperity to the kingdom. However, Dhritarashtra's own sons—the hundred Kauravas—were not happy in the least. They were worried that their cousins would now lay claim to the throne. Such was the Pandavas' first dramatic arrival to Hastinapur. But there is more…

The Pandavas were to have their own palace. This added to the Kauravas' fear, hatred and jealousy, leading them to hatch evil plans against their cousins. They wanted to kill the Pandavas and make it look like an accident. They bribed the architect to make their cousins' new palace with flammable material, so that they could set it on fire, killing the Pandava clan.

Thankfully, their uncle Vidur came to know of this nasty plot and warned the Pandavas before it was too late. Along with their mother Kunti, the five brothers escaped through a secret tunnel dug underneath the palace when it was set ablaze.

Thereafter, the five brothers lived in disguise and in much poverty. One day, they attended an archery contest in a nearby kingdom called Panchala. This competition (a practice called 'swayamvar') was organized to choose the worthiest groom for Princess Draupadi, daughter of King Drupad. Arjuna, who was the most skilled archer in the kingdom, passed the test with great ease, winning Draupadi's hand in marriage. When the brothers brought Draupadi back to their hut, they were eager to share the exciting news with Kunti. 'Look, Mother, what we have with us!' they shouted in unison. 'Whatever it is, you five brothers must share it,' Kunti said, unaware of Draupadi's presence. And that is how Draupadi came to have five husbands.

The news of Draupadi's marriage to the Pandavas soon spread like wildfire and reached Hastinapur. Dhritarashtra and his sons realized that the Pandavas were not dead after all. The king invited them home and thus, the Pandavas returned to Hastinapur for the second time. This time, Yudhishthira was even crowned the king of a part of their kingdom called Indraprastha.

However, their joy was short-lived. The Kauravas were not done wreaking havoc on the Pandavas. They engaged the Pandava brothers in a game of dice with their uncle Shakuni, who was a very skilled player. The Pandavas didn't stand a chance. They bet everything they had, including Draupadi, and lost!

The Kauravas gave them another chance—play again and win everything back. However, if the Pandavas lost, they would have to go away on exile again for thirteen years. This included one year of living anonymously. Unfortunately, the Pandavas lost again, thus forced to spend the next thirteen years in exile. This time, however, they realized that they would have to fight the Kauravas to stake their rightful claim to the throne.

At the end of their exile, they did not go to Hastinapur themselves. Their friend and ally Lord Krishna went on their behalf to broker peace. However, Duryodhana, the eldest and the most powerful of the Kauravas, was dead set against compromising with the Pandavas.

What followed was the legendary battle of Kurukshetra that lasted eighteen days. More than a hundred thousand foot soldiers were involved in the war. Many lives were lost on both sides. A war of that magnitude was being witnessed for the first time. This is why it is called the Mahabharata War or the Great Indian War. In the end, the Pandavas emerged victorious and they returned to Hastinapur with Yudhishthira as the rightful king. It was a joyous day for the entire kingdom.

But what is the epic's connection with Diwali? In the

> **A RAMAYANA CHARACTER CROSSOVER IN THE MAHABHARATA?**
>
> There are quite a few of these instances, but the most interesting one is of Hanuman. In the Mahabharata, he and Bhima have an encounter. At first, Bhima thinks he is just another monkey and only realizes his mistake when he fails to even lift the tail of Hanuman. Interestingly, they are brothers—as they are both sons of Vayu Dev, the God of Wind!

Ramayana, it is believed that Rama returned to Ayodhya on the eve of Diwali. In the Mahabharata, it is believed that the return of the Pandavas to Hastinapur occurred on the same night. The people of the kingdom lit rows of diyas outside their homes in anticipation of their homecoming. Interestingly, this return is said to be after their thirteen-year-long exile. But the Pandavas technically didn't return to Hastinapur immediately after their exile! They did so only after the end of the war.

Others believe that the great war of Mahabharata began on the evening of Diwali. Even today, in Himachal Pradesh, Diwali celebrations involve enacting scenes from the Mahabharata. People perform folk songs and dances associated with the epic—adventures in the forest, battles with evil and a victorious return home.

FOUR

The Oceanic Birth and the Wedding of Goddess Lakshmi

Diwali and Lakshmi Puja are celebrated together in most parts of India. In the East, Lakshmi Puja is celebrated on Sharad Purnima, the full moon night two weeks before Diwali. But everywhere else, it is celebrated on the third day of the five-day Diwali festival. As per Hindu mythology, Goddess Lakshmi wedded Lord Vishnu on this auspicious day.

The conclusion of this story is no doubt a happy one. However, the series of events that lead up to it is quite a thrilling adventure. It involves a curse, many gods and asuras, and the churning of the great ocean. You will come across the legend of Shiva's blue throat and also a divine swayamvar of sorts. Read on…

One day, Indra, the king of the heavens, was rude to Sage Durvasa, without realizing it. Indra wasn't careful with a gift given by the sage, which offended him. Durvasa was known for his powerful curses and short temper. As expected, the sage felt insulted and cursed all the gods in heaven to become weak. Indra apologized immediately, but to no avail.

When it rains, it pours. The powers of the legion of gods were already starting to deplete. Now, the asuras also attacked their homes. Indra had to run from pillar to post asking for help. Vishnu finally gave them the solution to their decreasing stamina and power—it was the quest for Amrita, the magical elixir of youth, immortality and power. The only problem was that it lay deep under the Ocean of Milk, among many other magical things and beings. Note that in Hindu cosmology, there were seven concentric oceans—the Ocean of Milk being the fifth, and it was mostly unexplored. The gods needed to churn the ocean and draw out the potion. For that, they needed a churner. After much deliberation, it was decided that the churner would have to be Mount Mandara. It would need to be plucked and carried to the ocean.

The gods were perplexed. Even at the height of their power, Mount Mandara was difficult to raise and in their weak condition, it was next to impossible. There was no way out; they would have to get the asuras involved. But how?

Vishnu guided the devas with a foolproof plan. First, they would have to get the asuras to agree to the plan. The asuras would most surely agree if they were promised their share of the potion. The next step would be to convince Vasuki, the Snake God, to be a part of it. They needed him to be the rope to entwine around the peak for the churning. In return, he would also receive a part of the potion. Vishnu advised the gods to ensure that they picked the tail end of Vasuki when they were finally ready. In answer to their puzzled looks, Vishnu winked and asked them to just have faith in him. They would soon find out the wisdom behind his cryptic suggestion.

Everything mostly went according to plan as there were a few hiccups. The asuras and Vasuki agreed to help out in the churning. They got Mount Mandara, but almost died in the process. As they had imagined, the mountain was intensely heavy. Even with the combined super-strength of the devas and the asuras, it was not an easy task. At one point, they could no longer carry it and it fell to the ground, crushing nearly half of them. Thankfully, it was Vishnu to the rescue! They were revived by him and came back doubly strong, and could finally lug the mountain to the ocean.

But there was no place to keep the churner and it kept sinking into the ocean. Well, it was Vishnu again who stepped in to help. He took on his second avatar of Kurma or the tortoise. He went and lay on the ocean and on his back the churner was placed with Vasuki wrapped around it.

Then Indra slyly went and announced in front of the asuras that the gods choose Vasuki's head side. The reverse psychology worked. The demons refused to let the gods get away with their choice of the snake's end and chose the tail end instead. What happened next? Let's find out.

First, the gods and demons threw different herbs into the ocean for better results. Once both sides started pulling at the snake, the churning of the great ocean or 'Samudra Manthan' began. The demons, to their dismay, discovered they had made a mistake. Every time they pulled Vasuki's head, he involuntarily spat up some venom. This fell on all their arms and burned them. But it was too late to switch tactics!

As the ocean churned, plenty of things started coming out of the ocean, and not all of them were pleasant. The first object to emerge was the poison Halahala, which started suffocating everyone around with its noxious fumes and threatened to destroy the entire world. Indra begged Shiva to help them and therefore with no other option left, Shiva drank the poison. Parvati, Shiva's wife, was shocked and would not let him swallow it. She grasped his throat so that it would not go down. The poison got arrested in his throat and turned it blue. This is why Lord Shiva is portrayed with a blue throat and is called Neelkanth.

VISHNU'S DIVINE TATTOO

Did you know that after Vishnu and Lakshmi got married, the former got the Srivatsa mark inked on his chest? It means 'beloved of Sri' and it is said that Lakshmi resides there, in his heart. That is not all. It is prophesied that Vishnu's tenth avatar, Kalki, will appear at the end of the Kali Yuga with the same mark on his chest.

The churning continued, with many other objects such as gems, supernatural animals, valuables and celestial beings being thrown up. Next to emerge was Lakshmi, who stunned everyone with her divine beauty. All the devas and asuras wanted her attention. Instead, as was customary, an impromptu swayamvar occurred. After surveying all her potential grooms, Lakshmi chose to marry Vishnu.

The wedding of Lakshmi and Vishnu was a key moment in Indian mythology. It occurred amidst the churning of the ocean, surrounded by all the devas and asuras. Today, we observe Lakshmi Puja to celebrate this holy union.

FIVE

King Vikramaditya's New Calendar

Before we start this interesting (and slightly confusing) chapter, here's an exercise. I want you to go ask the adults in your house how popular or common your name is. Why? Because this story will show you what happens when characters have the same name. It turns into a case of mistaken identity!

Well, thousands of years ago, Vikramaditya was quite a popular name for kings, leading to much confusion among historians. Ironically, Chandragupta Maurya II was actually more commonly known as Vikramaditya ('Sun of Power' in Sanskrit). Already confused? Don't be, we are just getting started! So buckle up, and listen to this.

More than a millennium ago, there was a king called

Vikramaditya, who grew up in the forest. This story begins with his father, the powerful King Gandharvasena of Ujjain, who once angered a Jain monk called Kalakacharya by abducting his sister Sarasvati. Power made kings accustomed to take by force whatever they desired, and it seems Gandharvasena was no different. Kalakacharya knew that if he had to rescue his sister, he would need someone's help. Therefore, he approached the king of the Shakas, a foreign tribe.

The Shakas agreed to help the monk. They attacked Gandharvasena, who, defeated, fled to the forest and the Shakas took over Ujjain. Sarasvati reunited with her brother. When King Gandharvasena's son, the young Vikramaditya, came of age, he decided to avenge his father's defeat and re-establish his reign in Ujjain. After a fierce battle, he emerged victorious. On the auspicious occasion of his coronation, Vikramaditya founded a calendar, which we know as Vikram Samvat, and Diwali marks the beginning of this calendar year.

Now, here is the interesting part. There was no mention of the name 'Vikramaditya' for centuries after the actual calendar came into being! It seems the calendar was known by a

> **THE ORIGINS OF BAITAL PACHISI**
>
> King Vikramaditya was such a legend—half-real and half-mythical—that it inspired Sanskrit scholars of yore to spin fantastical tales around him, including the twenty-five stories of King Vikram and the ghost Betaal.

completely different name earlier as well. It was called 'Krta' or 'Kritaa' and simply 'Samvat' (era). Now this could mean two things: first, the calendar was not founded by the original Vikramaditya and second, it was renamed by some other king who later renamed himself Vikramaditya! In any case, no historian is sure about the true identity of this second king. Yet, Vikram Samvat or the Hindu calendar, continues to be in use even today. The origin of Diwali is still connected to King Vikramaditya's new calendar. Even in present-day Gujarat and Rajasthan, the New Year falls on the day after Diwali. This is the first day of the month of Kartik and the first day of the Vikram Samvat calendar.

Part 2

The Five Days of Diwali

SIX

Day 1: Dhanteras | How King Hima's Wife Foiled Yama's Deadly Plans

The five days of Diwali are marked with specific pujas and each day has its own significance. Each of them stems from different legends and have their own special myths associated to it. The first day is known as Dhanatrayodashi or simply Dhanteras. It also has its own set of origin stories. Let's find out about them...

For most urban Hindu families, Dhanteras usually means shopping. It is the day you go to the market and buy precious metals or utensils. But do you know where that tradition stems from? It is an exciting adventure of a legend, but we will get to it a little later. First, let us try and understand what else Dhanteras entails.

For starters, 'Dhan' or 'Dhana' refers to Dhanvantari,

one of the avatars of Vishnu and the physician of the gods. 'Trayodashi' or 'Teras' refers to the thirteenth day of the dark fortnight of the Ashwin month.

Thus, when Hindus say that 'health is wealth', they have entire legends to back their claim. On the one hand, Dhanteras is celebrated by worshipping Lakshmi and Kuber—the female and male deities of wealth. This is because the churning of the ocean gave birth to Lakshmi, the goddess of prosperity. This day is also celebrated as the National Ayurveda Day or Dhanvantari Divas. It is believed that Dhanvantari too emerged from the ocean on this day of Samudra Manthan, carrying the book of Ayurveda in one hand and the elixir of immortality or Amrita, in the other.

This day is celebrated through the country through different customs and traditions. Some offer prayers to Ganesha too. Offerings of puffed rice, rice cakes and sugar candies are made to the deities. Communities involved in Ayurveda perform special havan rituals to worship the god of health! In rural areas, farmers worship their cattle. In South India, a traditional medicinal concoction is prepared and consumed. And in cities everywhere, jewellery, hardware and utensil stores do brisk business.

Of course, it is auspicious to bring home precious metals on the day we pray to Lakshmi. But there is another legend from Hindu mythology that feeds this annual ritual. And it all begins with a prophecy of the death of a king.

A very long time ago, there was a king named Hima, who had a son with a death prophecy in his natal chart. It was foretold that he would die on the fourth night of his marriage from a snakebite. Despite this prediction, the prince got married at the age of sixteen. When his new bride came to know of this curse, she was determined to change her husband's destiny.

On the fourth night of their wedding, the young couple lay awake. The wife devised a plot to foil the prophecy. She collected all her jewellery and all the gold and silver coins they had and put them in a huge heap right outside their sleeping chamber. Additionally, she lit several lamps, filling the space with a blinding brightness and shimmer.

Once that was done, she retired to their unlit sleeping chamber with her prince. She sat up all night, narrating stories and singing songs to him, so that he did not doze off. What happened in the meantime was that Yama, the God of Death, arrived at their home in the guise of a snake to take away the prince's soul, just as was foretold in his horoscope.

> **KEEPING THE GOD OF DEATH HAPPY**
>
> An important ritual performed on Dhanteras is the lighting of a lamp in the southern direction in one's backyard. Known by different names such as Jam ka Diya, Yama Deepam or Yama Dipadana, this lamp is supposed to be made of atta (flour) and filled with sesame oil. It is thought to appease Yamraj, the God of Death, and keep him away from one's home which basically means to stop untimely death of a family member.

Blinded by the dazzle of the precious metals and diyas, all Yama, in his reptilian body, could do was climb atop the heap of precious metal. He sat listening to the sounds of tales and songs coming from the inner chambers. When the sun came up next morning, the snake simply slithered away. The princess was able to change her husband's destiny. Henceforth, this magical night came to be observed as Dhanteras.

And that is the myth behind the buying of precious metals on this auspicious day. It is a ritual rooted in the belief that doing so will keep misfortune at bay and bring good luck. That is why people buy gold and silver coins, jewellery and kitchen utensils on Dhanteras.

SEVEN

Day 2: How Krishna Freed 16,000 Princesses from the Evil King Narakasura

> Diwali has another mythical origin anecdote with all the essential elements of a great story. An ambitious villain, his rise to power and the desire to be immortal. The kidnapping of princesses, the chosen one's heroic entry and a surprising twist in the end. This tale begins with an asura from the North-East called Narakasura.

Once upon a time, Vishnu assumed his third avatar of Varaha or the boar. In that avatar, his horn once touched Bhudevi, the Goddess of Earth, and thus, she conceived his son, who was born as Narakasura or Naraka. He grew up to become the founder of the Bhauma dynasty of Pragjyotisha Kamarupa (present-day Guwahati). At that time,

> ### HOW A ROOSTER FOILED NARAKA'S WEDDING PLANS
>
> Narakasura, besides the infamous kidnapping, is also known for his proposal to Goddess Kamakhya. She did not think it was wise to outrightly say no, so she set him an impossible task: to build a staircase from the foot of the Nilachal Hills to her temple atop within one night. Narakasura would have almost completed the challenge, but Kamakhya tricked him by strangling a rooster till he crowed, which indicated that it was dawn. This made Naraka believe that he had failed. The incomplete staircase is called Mekhelauja Path and can still be found on the way up to the Kamakhya Temple in Guwahati.

it included the rest of Assam as well as some neighbouring states and even countries.

When Narakasura started out to fulfil his ambitions of conquest, he asked Brahma for the boon of immortality. Brahma, however, refused to grant him that boon as death was inevitable for anyone and everyone. So Naraka went about it in a more subtle manner and asked that his death should only be at his mother's hand. Brahma granted his boon and, combined with his great powers, Naraka became undefeatable. He conquered all the kingdoms on earth and from all these conquered kingdoms, he kidnapped sixteen thousand women.

Some say they were princesses, others claim they were the daughters of gods, kings, asuras and sages. Some others even say that they were heavenly maidens. Narakasura kept them imprisoned on top of Maniparvata, a mountain in his kingdom. A five-headed demon and his sons guarded the women. Interestingly, Maniparvata mountain is said to have been a part of the mountain containing the Sanjeevani, the herb Hanuman had carried with him to revive Lakshmana, who had been grievously injured in the war against Ravana in the Ramayana.

Meanwhile, Narakasura, not being content, started targeting the kingdom of heaven. Even Indra, the King of Heaven, could not keep him out. He had to flee along with the other celestial beings residing there. Narakasura stole the glowing earrings of Aditi, the mother of all celestial deities. Another item taken was the umbrella of Varuna, the God of Oceans. When the devas went to complain to Vishnu, he promised to vanquish the asura. For this, he would have to be born on earth in his eighth avatar. Meanwhile, Narakasura's reign of terror lasted a long time.

Vishnu was finally incarnated as Krishna on earth. As per the plans set in motion in heaven, Aditi then went to complain to her relative Satyabhama, one of Krishna's wives. She was livid and urged Krishna to act against the asura king. He agreed and asked her to come along. They mounted the golden-winged bird Garuda and flew to Narakasura's great fortress, where a fierce battle ensued.

Narakasura unleashed lakhs of foot soldiers, battle elephants and horses on Krishna. He also let loose on him divine super weapons. Krishna destroyed and deflected each of them with much ease. However, despite Krishna's best efforts, Narakasura was invincible, thanks to his boon from Brahma.

Now, the ending of this tale has two versions. In one version, Krishna finally used his Sudarshan Chakra to kill Narakasura. This falls in line with Vishnu's earlier promise. There is another version which is probably more exciting. When Krishna was hurt in one of the attacks, a helpless and enraged Satyabhama shot an arrow at Narakasura.

Remember how Narakasura was protected by his boon? How his death could only happen at the hands of his mother, Bhudevi? Now, Satyabhama was an avatar of Mother Earth herself, so her arrow killed Narakasura. Krishna then opened his eyes, smiling mischievously. He knew all along that Narakasura's death was supposed to occur at the hands of his wife.

It is said that before he died, the king requested a boon from Satyabhama—that his death should not be forgotten but celebrated every year with lights. Thus, was born Naraka Chaturdashi, the second day of Diwali.

All the stolen goods were returned to their rightful owners and peace was restored on heaven and earth. But what about the sixteen thousand princesses? Well, they begged Krishna to keep them with him as his wives. Krishna agreed. And that is how Krishna came to have so many wives. According to another legend, these princesses were the daughters of a king. They had received a boon, that in their next life, they would become the wives of the god Vishnu.

After the war, Krishna and Satyabhama went back to

their home. Right before daybreak, they cleaned up with sandalwood paste and scented oils before taking a bath. To this date, people take an oil bath on the dawn of Diwali.

EIGHT

Day 2: Why Hanuman Is Worshipped before Rama

The second day of Diwali has several names. You can call it Chhoti Diwali or Little Diwali because it is the day before Diwali. It is called Naraka Chaturdashi ('Chaturdashi' meaning fourteenth). It falls on the fourteenth day of the dark fortnight of the Ashwin month. This was the day the asura king Narakasura was killed by Satyabhama.

In some parts of India such as Gujarat and Rajasthan, this day is also called Kali Chaudas. Here, it is believed that it was Kali who killed the evil Narakasura. 'Kali' here also means dark or eternal and 'Chaudas' again refers to fourteen. As such, it is the most important day to worship Mahakali or Shakti.

This is a night that is heavy with the idea, if not the presence, of the supernatural. Kajal is applied to ward off the evil eye. Those getting initiated into Hindu occult studies or tantrism start to learn the mantras on this day. Families wake up before dawn to take a ritualistic bath known as Abhyanga Snan. It is a bathing ritual that includes a full body massage with a special ayurvedic mixture. In western India, this mixture is made up of various herbs and spices known as ubtan, whereas in southern India, it consists of besan (gram flour), oil and sandalwood powder. It is supposed to have plenty of health benefits. Symbolically, this holy bath is believed to destroy the evil within us. In Goa, people burn effigies of Narakasura before taking this bath, which symbolically denotes the destruction of evil.

In West Bengal and among the Bengali community elsewhere, this night is observed as Bhoot Chaturdashi. Spooky, right? It is believed that the veil separating the underworld from our world is quite thin. On this night, the gateway to the other world opens, allowing the spirits of our ancestors—technically speaking, fourteen—to come visit us from the land of the dead. Thus, fourteen diyas are lit to show them the way. It is very much like the animation movie *Coco*! The movie is about a similar ritual followed in Mexico, where a special day called the Day of the Dead is celebrated.

But wait a minute! What does all of this have to do with Hanuman? Well, it was important to first describe the type of otherworldly activity associated with this night. Now, its relation to Hanuman can be revealed.

Hanuman, whose celestial father is Vayu or the God of Wind, is also known as Pawanputra. Remember when we were earlier talking about how this day is celebrated in various ways with many names? Well, this day is also observed as Hanuman Puja. Hanuman is the deity of protection, power and strength, and thus, Hindus invoke him on this day to seek protection from evil spirits that may be around.

Second, according to some, Hanuman was born on this day. But there are some who celebrate his birthday or Hanuman Jayanti on different days. For instance, in Maharashtra, it is on the full moon day of the Hindu month of Chaitra. The story of his birth is as interesting as the tales of heroism around this deity.

This story involves some godly payasam or rice pudding. The payasam was divinely received by Dasharatha of Ayodhya. He was blessed with it after performing a sacred ritual to

> **BODY PAINTING IN DEVOTION**
>
> Legend has it that when Hanuman saw Sita applying *sindur* or vermilion on her forehead, he asked her about its significance. She said that doing so would ensure her husband Rama's long life. Hanuman then smeared his entire body with vermilion in a symbolic manner to demonstrate his devotion to his Lord and ensure his immortality. And that is why Hanuman idols are usually vermilion-coloured, to depict the Rambhakt's devotion.

help his wives conceive. He was carrying it to his three wives when some of it was snatched by a kite flying by. It accidentally fell on an apsara called Anjana. She was cursed to live on earth till she gave birth to a son. She herself was praying for a child when the payasam fell on her open palms. She ate it and that's how Hanuman was conceived.

The final myth behind the worship of Hanuman on Naraka Chaturdashi goes like this. Rama was very pleased with Hanuman's devotion, right from the Lanka mission for rescuing Sita. Hanuman went out of his way to serve Rama in his mission. He flew to Lanka and battled a whole army of demons. He played the messenger between Rama and Sita. He carried an entire mountain to help revive the war-injured Lakshmana with the Sanjeevani herb growing on it. He even became Rama's envoy to Ayodhya, rushing back to the kingdom to bring the news of Rama's return.

Diwali is celebrated to mark Rama's return to Ayodhya. But Rama blessed Hanuman to be worshipped before him. Therefore, Hanuman Puja is organized a day before the celebration of Rama's return.

NINE

Day 3: How Goddess Kali Almost Destroyed the World

Most of India celebrates Diwali and Lakshmi Puja on the third day of Diwali. However, that is not the case in East India, especially West Bengal and among Bengali communities across the country, where they worship the Goddess of time and power, creation and destruction—Kali, one of the most fascinating Hindu goddesses. With her dark-blue skin, frightening expressions and appearance, and an aura of wrath, she gets a bad reputation. Did you know that Kali is said to have as many as twenty-one avatars? They range from the more popular destructive goddess to that of a nurturing and protective mother.

Although Kali is the fierce feminine energy that embodies the power of destruction, it is the destruction of evil. It is not only perfectly acceptable, but also required to restore balance in the universe. But when this energy goes a little out of hand, it can potentially be harmful. And that is where this famous legend comes from.

The story begins with the asura Raktabija, along with two others Shumbha and Nishumbha. They were involved in a huge war with Maa Kaushiki, the warrior form of Goddess Parvati. She and the group of mother goddesses together called the Matrikas battled against the asuras. In Hindu mythology, clashes between gods and demons are depicted as going on since eternity; they were always at war with each other. These asuras in particular had earned the wrath of the goddesses for taking away the homes of the gods in heaven.

Maa Kaushiki succeeded in killing Shumbha and Nishumbha in the fierce fight, but Raktabija had a special power which made him almost invincible. His name literally meant 'seed of blood' ('Rakta' or blood and 'Bija' or seed). Thus, more Raktabijas came into being from every drop of his blood that spilled on the battleground, making it nearly impossible to defeat him.

No matter how hard the goddesses tried to kill him, they couldn't. The spawning of new Raktabijas meant that pretty soon the entire battlefield was full of his clone army. It became clear that it was impossible to defeat the demon on their own. So, Goddess Parvati or Devi Kaushiki summoned the most powerful and destructive of all goddesses—Kali.

From Parvati's frown in the middle of her forehead burst

forth Kali. Imagine how movies and comics portray the entry of a superhero (or heroine)—dramatic, right! A garland of skulls draped around her neck, dressed in tiger skin, burning red eyes, with mouth open and tongue out, Kali was the epitome of fury. She was armed with a sword, noose and a *khatvanga* or a stick topped with a skull. Kali roared, attacking the enemy.

She devoured all the Raktabijas and then collected the blood of the real asura in a bowl as the other goddesses slayed him. Even though the battle was won, Kali's bloodlust had just been awakened. It is said that she was enraged at the evil among the asuras and even humans so much so that she continued on her path of annihilation. She could not see cause and effect; she just knew that all she wanted to do was purge the universe of all evil.

The destructive energy she had unleashed on the battlefield could not be contained. The gods became concerned that if she did not stop, she would end up destroying the entire universe. They went to Shiva to beg him to somehow put an end to the unstoppable force of Kali. It is believed that Shiva tried to get Kali to listen, but her attention was unattainable. So, the only thing he could do in the end was to lie down on Kali's path to stop her rush of fury.

Kali did not see Shiva lying on her path and stepped on him to charge ahead. When she felt him under her foot, she looked down and immediately stopped. She bit her tongue out of sheer embarrassment and regret. This is the moment frozen by artists in graphic visualization of this goddess.

There is another take on this myth. Some believe that Shiva lay down in her path to receive her grace, almost like a devotee hoping to receive moksha. In any case, Shiva was the only one who was able to stop Kali from destroying the universe completely.

In contrast to her reputation, Bengali households worship the benevolent Dakshinakali. Dakshina means the gift given to priests before any puja. Thus, this form of Kali is also depicted with her right hands in gestures of gifting and blessing. The Goddess is a motherly one, even called Kali Maa.

Another version of the legend of Dakshinakali also exists. It refers to the other meaning of Dakshin, which means 'south'. The God of Death, Yama, is said to have lived in the south. Apparently, he fled in terror upon hearing Kali's name. Hence, the belief is that anyone who worships Dakshinakali will be able to beat death!

> **BEST FOOT FORWARD?**
>
> Goddess Kali is worshipped both by tantriks as well as priests and regular people. But how do you differentiate which Kali is worshipped by who? Look at the foot of Kali on Shiva's body. If it is the left foot, it is the form of Vamakali, the more dangerous and destructive Kali that is worshipped by tantriks. The Kali with her right foot is Dakshinakali, the gentler form of Kali revered in Bengali households. That is because the left is always associated with transgression.

TEN

Day 4: Govardhan Puja or Annakut | How Krishna Saved Braj Villagers by Lifting a Mountain

The day after Diwali, or the fourth day of Diwali, is of significance. Mythical adventures and legends abound this day. It is celebrated as Govardhan Puja or Annakut. In fact, in Gujarat, it is considered New Year's Day. What is the importance of this day in Hindu mythology? Well, it involves an angry Indra, a powerful Krishna and many thankful villagers.

Our story begins in the famous region of Gokul-Braj in Uttar Pradesh. Krishna is said to have had many adventures growing up here. In the middle of the region is a hillock called Govardhan Hill or Giri, near which lived many cowherds. Every autumn, they would worship

Indra, the mighty king of gods who was also the god of rain and storm. It was an attempt to appease the god.

Now, Krishna might have been a young cowherd himself during this story, but everyone in Gokul had a lot of faith in him and respected him for his wisdom and power. One day, he pointed out that people should stop offering prayers to Indra. They should instead be worshipping Govardhan Hill. Krishna had a fair point. After all, it was the hillock that provided them with natural resources for their livelihood. It had grass for the cattle's food, trees for their shelter and natural beauty. All the natural phenomena around the hillock occurred because of it.

The villagers were convinced and decided to start worshipping the hill instead. Indra, who was witnessing all this, felt scorned. How dare they shift their loyalties at the mere mention by Krishna? Did they not know how powerful the God of Storm and Thunder can be? Well, they need to be taught a lesson, Indra decided.

Hence, Indra sent forth thunderstorms and rains to Gokul. It was no ordinary thunderstorm; it was cursed with divine wrath. The people were helpless, they did not know what to do or where to go. However, Lord Krishna was there for them. He did something similar to what Hanuman did after the Ramayana war. He picked up the entire Govardhan hill, and that too on the little finger of his left hand! Hanuman did a similar thing when he had to get the Sanjeevani herb to revive the slain Lakshmana.

All the people and cattle took shelter under it while the skies above raged. For seven days and seven nights, relentless

> **DISHING OUT RECORDS ON ANNAKUT**
>
> Did you know that the Shri Swaminarayan Mandir in the UK holds the Guinness World Record for the largest Annakut, in which 1,247 vegetarian dishes were prepared and offered to the gods, in 2000? In fact, the magnificence of this festival can also be gauged from the *chhappan bhog* or fifty-six dishes traditionally offered to the deities.

rain and thunder lashed the city of Gokul. However, the inhabitants were safely tucked under their blessed hillock. Krishna asked everyone to share whatever food they had with each other to sustain themselves during this period. In the end, even Indra conceded defeat to Krishna and stopped the devastating storm.

This happened on the fourth day of Diwali. Hindus in west, central and north India celebrate it as Govardhan Puja and Annakut. Govardhan Puja is the worship of the hillock, which is now a pilgrimage site for devotees. Annakut refers to a mountain of food or grains. It is specially made on this occasion and offered to the deities. Dozens of dishes are prepared with every possible vegetarian ingredient. They are cooked on the days leading up to the festival. In fact, Annakut is also a day when vegetarian food is emphasized upon. There is a special dish called Annakut Sabzi as well. After all, this is a harvest festival too. By this time, the harvest is done and winter is just around the corner. And any agricultural activity is incomplete without cattle. Hence, as part of the rituals, cow dung is used to make mountain-like miniatures, which are then worshipped after placing diyas in front of them.

The festivities are observed by offering food to the deities, observing fast and singing hymns. The fast is broken with a little bit of the food that was offered to the gods. Doing so is considered auspicious. And thus ends the fourth day of Diwali.

ELEVEN

Day 4: How Vishnu Tricked King Bali and Sent Him to Netherworld

If you had the superpower to transform into anything, what would you choose? And most importantly, what would you do in that avatar? Lord Vishnu had at least ten avatars. He has been instrumental in changing the course of particular narratives in Hindu mythology in several ways. This legend involves one of his many avatars as well as a powerful king and an interesting turn of events.

The story begins with King Mahabali or Bali, the grandson of Prahlad. Prahlad's father Hiranyakashipu was killed by another one of Vishnu's avatars, Narasimha. Now, keep in mind, Bali might have been an asura king, but he was an upright and benevolent one. He was loved by his people, as proven in the scriptures. However, he had a bad reputation. His fellow asuras were always causing trouble for the devas.

Remember, this is the same Mahabali who was present during the Samudra Manthan. He had tasted Amrita or the elixir of immortality churned out of the ocean. Although the devas and asuras came together this once, the fight between them continued. Eventually, Bali won control of the entire heaven and earth. And it wasn't long before the devas had enough of the asuras' antics.

Apparently, Bali was also extremely devoted to Vishnu. And this became a problem when the devas approached the god. They wanted his help in defeating the asuras led by Bali in the never-ending war between them. Vishnu refused to defeat Bali outright because he was pleased with Bali's devotion. However, he also had to do his duties and help the other devas. It was a dilemma, but when there's a god, there's a way! Vishnu decided to use one of the many tricks up his sleeve.

It so happened that King Bali announced that he would be performing a yagna (ritual). If anyone asked for any favours during this ritual,

> **ORIGINAL HOME OF THE KING OF THE WORLD?**
>
> While it is usually accepted that the origin of Mahabali lies in Kerala, there are other places that lay claims to the king; for instance, Balia in Uttar Pradesh, Mahabaleshwar in Maharashtra, Bharuch in Gujarat and Mahabalipuram in Tamil Nadu.

he would be granted those. And this is where Vishnu took his chance. He took on his fifth avatar—that of a dwarf Brahman called Vamana. He approached Bali, who offered him riches and villages, horses and elephants.

However, Vamana demurred, saying all he needed was the rights over whatever area he can cover in three steps. It was a measly amount of land to a king who ruled over such vast territories. Smug in his ignorance about being set up by the very god he worshipped, Bali agreed, and what happened next is the stuff of legends.

Once he had Bali's consent, Vishnu, in the guise of Vamana, grew to humongous proportions. In just one step, he covered the entire earth and in the next, he covered the heavens. There was nothing else to walk on! Remember how Bali was very upright? Well, Bali meant to keep up his end of the promise. For Vamana's final step, he offered him his own head. And that's when Vishnu had him. He pushed him into the netherworld and made him the king of Patal Lok. Vishnu also granted him a boon: Bali could come back to earth once a year to be worshipped by his people.

And thus, the fourth day of Diwali is celebrated in honour of King Bali's return to this world for a day. This day is called Balipratipada ('Bali' for the name of the king and 'pratipada' meaning 'occasion'). It has other names too such as Bali Padyami, Padva, Virapratipada and Dyutapratipada. It is also called Barlaj in Himachal Pradesh. In Jammu, it is known as Raja Bali and it is celebrated as Onam in Kerala. This important day is marked by the making of rangoli designs, lighting lamps and exchanging gifts. Icons or images of Bali are made with cow dung. These are then decorated with kolam designs and flowers and worshipped.

TWELVE

Day 5: Bhai Dooj | The Happy Reunion of Krishna and His Sister Subhadra

Hindus celebrate the relationship between brothers and sisters in a grand manner. There are even holidays for it!
And these holidays, of course, stem from traditions that find their roots in the mythical past. Raksha Bandhan is definitely one of them, but here, we will talk about the original legend of Bhai Dooj.

It is celebrated on the fifth and final day of Diwali. On this day, sisters shower their love and blessings on their brothers. Bhai Dooj—called thus in north India—goes by different names. It depends on which region you belong to. It is Bhaubeej in west India, Bhai Tika among Nepalis and Bhai Phonta among Bengalis. Some other regional variations are Bhardutiya in Bihar and Bhai Jiuntia in Odisha. In Andhra

Pradesh and Telengana, it is Bhatri Ditya or Bhagini Hastha Bhojanam. It has more names, but we shall get to it later.

'Bhai' as you know means brother and 'Dooj' or 'Beej' means the second. Here, it means the second day of the bright fortnight of the Kartik month. Tika and Phonta alternatively mean the mark that is put on the forehead during the ceremony. So, where did this ritual come from? To find out, we have to go a few chapters and thousands of years back.

Remember when Krishna had battled with the evil king Narakasura to rescue sixteen thousand princesses from his lair? It is said that after he won, Krishna went to meet his sister Subhadra. It was a happy meeting for the siblings, as Subhadra welcomed Krishna with flowers and sweets. She did aarti and applied a tika of vermilion paste on his forehead. Krishna was very pleased with this reception and blessed her with many boons, it is believed. And that's how and why Bhai Dooj continues to be celebrated.

What is even more interesting is that Krishna and Subhadra were stepbrother and sister! While both shared the same father, Vasudeva, Krishna's birth mother was Devaki while Subhadra's was Rohini. So, Krishna was Subhadra's brother from another mother, as the saying goes.

As per the Bhai Dooj ceremony, sisters present gifts to their brothers, cook their favourite dishes and pray for their long life. There are still certain variations of this tradition.

> **NOT HIS SISTER'S KEEPER!**
>
> While Bhai Dooj might be celebrated in honour of Krishna and Subhadra, did you know that Krishna helped Arjuna abduct Subhadra? While it is believed that Krishna, in his infinite wisdom, did it for the benefit of the Pandavas in the great Mahabharata war, it certainly does not seem like a very brotherly thing to do!

In West Bengal, sisters apply a mark of curd, rice and kohl on their brothers' forehead. In Haryana and Maharashtra, women who do not have brothers worship the moon god, Chandra. Guess this is why the moon is lovingly called Chanda Mama (uncle or mother's brother).

Well, there are more myths of other gods related to the celebration of Bhai Dooj. Remember when I mentioned that there are more names to this festival? Well, one of them is Yama Dwitiya. Yama, as we all know by now, is the Hindu god of the underworld and 'Dwitiya' means the second. Legend has it, that Yama also returned to his twin sister, Yamuna or Yami. She welcomed him with a tilak on this day. They shared a meal and exchanged gifts. Yama declared that whoever gets a tilak from their sister on this auspicious day will get to stay further apart from death. And thus, it is marked to celebrate the bond between a brother and a sister.

So, be it any legend that you believe in, this day is very sacred. No matter how much we may fight or disagree, our siblings are important to us. And with this day of love and affectionate between brothers and sisters, the five days of Diwali come to an end.

Part 3

Beyond Hindus and India

THIRTEEN

The Day Lord Mahavira Attained Nirvana

Diwali is a very important Hindu or Indian festival, but it is celebrated by other religions and countries as well. And one of these religions is Jainism. The founder of the religion is Mahavira (meaning 'great hero'), who achieved nirvana on the day before Diwali, around 2,500 years ago! In Jainism, 'nirvana' means breaking out of the circle of life and death and becoming one with the universe. Let's hear his story.

Mahavira is the twenty-fourth and final tirthankara or spiritual teacher among the Jains. But he did not start out in life as a spiritual teacher. In fact, he was a prince of a district named Vaishali in Bihar! But he gave up his wealth, a luxurious life and his relationships in search of a higher purpose and went away to practise a spiritual life when he was around thirty years old. For twelve years, he fasted and meditated very strictly to gain greater spiritual knowledge.

One day, as he sat meditating under a Sal tree, he gained infinite knowledge. Do you know who is said to have infinite knowledge? Well, other than Google, it is apparently the omniscient God. In Jainism, this knowledge is called Keval Gyana. So, what he achieved was godhood, in a very specific sense. Since then, he began giving sermons to his followers.

And just like all living things die, it was also time for Mahavira's life on earth to come to an end. He spent thirty years of his life teaching. But unlike normal living beings, when Mahavira died, he achieved nirvana. It is said that he was meditating at the dawn of a new moon in Pawapuri, Bihar, when it happened. There are plenty of legends around it. Some say that heavenly bodies descended on earth to perform the last rites. The entire scene was lit up with their glowing presence.

> **HOW NON-VIOLENT ARE YOU?**
> Certainly not as much as Mahavira, who taught his followers not to touch or disturb any living being, swim, light a fire or even wave arms in the air, in case they accidentally harm a living organism.

It is also believed that when Jain spiritual leaders die, their whole body disappears into thin air! According to some accounts, on the sixth day of a sermon, the sleeping crowd woke up to find that Mahavira was not there—except his hair and nails, which they cremated.

The next night was pitch black. Thus, people lit up diyas in a symbolic manner. This was to keep the light of his learning alive even after he had moved on. Thus, its connection to Diwali is even deeper. In fact, one of the oldest mentions of Diwali is in the eighth century. It was a very similar word, Dipalikaya. It means 'light leaving the body', which signifies the passing away of Mahavira.

Today, Jains celebrate Diwali by offering Nirvan Ladoo in temples. Since they believe in non-violence, they do not burst crackers. Some observe fasting in memory of Mahavira. Rice and mustard are sprinkled after prayers to banish negativity. And with the next day—Pratipada—the Jain New Year begins.

FOURTEEN

The Day Guru Hargobind Helped 52 Kings Escape from Jail

Diwali is a special day for everyone, but it is extra special for Sikhs. On this day, the sixth Sikh Guru, Guru Hargobind, helped fifty-two princes and kings escape from jail in Gwalior Fort. This special day is called Bandi Chhor Divas. It is a very fascinating story that teaches you how to find the solution to any problem just by thinking outside the box.

The story begins with Guru Hargobind being made the sixth Guru of the Sikhs. This came after the Mughal emperor, Jahangir, killed his father Guru Arjan Dev. He died a martyr in 1606 for refusing to convert to Islam. The young Hargobind, crowned at the tender age of eleven, took his new role seriously. He even wore two swords: one for the spirit and another for the body. He had a militaristic outlook and was against the oppression by the Mughal rulers.

He built the Akal Takht, the Throne of the Almighty, in Amritsar. It is still an important seat of power for Sikhs. He also started strengthening the Sikh army. This began to worry the Mughal rulers. Jahangir was informed, who sent one of his officers, Wazir Khan, to arrest him. But Khan was a fan of Guru Hargobind, so he did not use violence. Instead, he lied to Guru Hargobind that Jahangir only wanted to meet him.

> **ARMED AND READY FOR BATTLE**
>
> The Nihang or Akali, which means immortal, is a warrior order of the Sikhs that are said to have originated from the Akali Dal (army of the immortal) started by Guru Hargobind himself. There are many orders of the Nihang, and on Bandi Chhor Divas, they display their martial arts in Amritsar, Punjab.

Luckily, on meeting Guru Hargobind, Jahangir was impressed by him. Instead of arresting Guru Hargobind, Jahangir invited him to a grand reception and then took him hunting. During this hunt, Guru Hargobind saved the emperor from a lion attack, and the incident made them good friends. But this also made many of Jahangir's courtiers jealous. They wanted to get rid of Guru Hargobind. One day, the emperor fell ill and an evil revenue official in his court took his chance. He tricked Guru Hargobind into travelling to the Gwalior Fort. He said that his stay there would be auspicious for the king's health, according to his astrological charts.

The fort turned out to be a jail where he had to remain for several months. During his imprisonment, he gained the love and respect of the dozens of detained prisoners, including several Rajput kings. When the emperor's health improved, he was finally allowed to be released. But he refused to leave the jail without taking with him all the princes and kings who were held there. Jahangir obviously would not let that happen. But Khan reminded him that he owes his life to Guru Hargobind.

So, a deal was worked out. The Guru could leave the jail with only those prisoners who could walk out holding on to his chola or robe. When he was informed of this, he was delighted. He knew just how he could get away with rescuing all the princes and kings. He immediately got a special chola made by his tailor with a long tail bearing fifty-two panels. He wore the robe, and fifty-two princes followed him, twenty-six on each side, holding onto one panel each!

And that is why this special day is called Bandi Chhor Divas ('Bandi' means 'prisoners', 'chhor' means 'release' and divas is 'a special day'). The people of Amritsar were happy seeing their Guru return after so long. Also, it happened to be Diwali. So, they lit many diyas, floating lamps and candles. Today, Sikhs celebrate this day by lighting their homes, performing *nagar kirtan* or processional hymns and organizing *langar* or communal meals.

FIFTEEN

The Day You Worship Yourself!

So far, you have read about the worship of several gods and goddesses. You are going to find out about the worship of several creatures also as you continue reading through this book. But right now, we are at a point where we are going to talk about a unique puja. Here, the object of worship is not some divine being, but the person themselves. Let me introduce you to Mha Puja, celebrated by the Newar community of Nepal.

'Mha' means oneself or one's body. Mha Puja is part of the five-day Swanti festival. It is the Newari version of Diwali in India or Tihar in Nepal. It is a day to purify and empower one's soul and is observed on the Nepali New Year's Day. It is usually carried out on the dining room floor. Mandalas for every family member are made separately. The ingredients used are lentils, grains, vermilion, flowers and other materials. Each item is used to make a concentric circle, which signifies completion. The mandala symbolizes the world and each item used is symbolic. For instance, the grains represent appeal for a long life, contentment and knowledge.

Three extra mandalas are made for the God of Life, the God of Death and the House God. Additionally, important items of the house also get a mandala of their own; for instance, the broom, water pot and bamboo tray. The entire ceremony is conducted by a senior woman of the household.

Everyone sits cross-legged in front of their mandala. They are given dabs of coloured paste on their foreheads. A long wick called *itaa*, and fruits which include citron are placed in front of them. It is believed that the longer the wick burns, the longer the person's life will be. And citron symbolizes a long and prosperous life.

The next part is called Sagan Biyegu. Members apply dabs of curd on their temples. They are then given sagun (which includes fruits, fried eggs, smoked fish, meat and a local Newari wine called *aila*). The wine bowl cannot be set on the ground before it has been refilled three times.

The ceremony ends with a feast. The food is also arranged like a mandala. The rice is served in the middle and surrounded by eight different foods. They represent the eight goddesses that are worshipped as protectors. The plate is set on top of the mandala. This destroys the design slightly and signifies that life is temporary.

FOOD FROM ALL ELEMENTS!
Each food item offered during Mha Puja has a symbolic nature. Eggs are food from creatures of the air and fish from the water. This symbolically means taking in all the knowledge of the world from top of the ground to below the ground—encompassing everything in between.

However, for the Newaris, the soul or the inner self never dies. The soul of each one of us carries within itself the very essence of God. And thus, Mha Puja is a very significant and unique ritual found only among the Newars of Nepal. The rest of the world, too, participates in the tradition of New Year resolution, but Mha Puja is an actual ceremony to rejuvenate the soul for the coming year.

SIXTEEN

Why Do Sindhis Tap Coins against Their Teeth on Diwali?

Just like the rest of India, the Sindhi community too celebrates Diwali with full rigour and tradition. However, they have some unique rituals. One of them is tapping gold or silver coins against their teeth during this festival. Quite interesting, isn't it? We will find out why, but first let us see what else Sindhis do during Diwali festivities.

For starters, this festival is known as Diyari in the Sindhi language. Among the delicious festive food they prepare, jaggery and peanut sweets called chikki deserve special mention. Another dish is Sai Bhaji, a high-protein vegetarian dish made of gram dal and spinach and eaten with rice.

There is a lot of symbolism in Sindhi Diyari rituals also.

They keep three matkas or pots in their homes filled with nuts, dried fruits and sweets, which symbolize the need to save. Another symbolic item for them is a hatri or a miniature house-shaped structure made from cow dung and clay. It is painted, decorated and installed with miniature idols of Lakshmi. This hatri symbolizes their shop, and Diwali is a time for praying for prosperity. Thus, they worship the Lakshmi kept inside.

> **BROOMSTICK BOYCOTT**
>
> Sindhis do not touch broomsticks or do any cleaning on the day of Diwali—hence they clean up and decorate their homes way in advance and prepare for the festivities accordingly.

Coming to the Lakshmi Puja rituals, Sindhis prepare a special thali. All the puja essentials such as rice and flowers are kept on it, swastikas are made with vermilion. Silver and gold coins are washed with raw milk and kept in the thali, which is then offered for puja. Once the aarti is over, the family members take one coin each from the thali. They then gently tap it against their teeth. While doing it, they say, '*Lakshmi aai, danat vaai*', meaning 'Lakshmi has come, poverty has gone away'.

The symbolism here is that no matter how much wealth you crave or have, you cannot really eat it. In this ritual is thus hidden a very practical lesson, which the people relearn every Diwali. Money is not the end but the means to a fulfilment and that there is more to life than wealth.

Another important symbolic ritual is that the male members of the family burn two *juaris* or sorghum stalks. They do it against the wall of their house after their meals. This signifies the harvest-ready status of the cereal crop.

Part 4

Celebrations Around the Country

SEVENTEEN

How Odisha Observes Halloween on Diwali

Have you heard of Halloween? If you have, you probably associate it with American kids getting dressed in scary or funny costumes. They go 'trick-or-treating' and fill the house with spooky decor. However, did you know that the original Halloween started out with bellmen of European towns dressed in black? They went around ringing bells and asking people to pray for the dead. Soul cakes were given out in exchange for prayers, which is considered the origin of the 'trick-or-treat' custom.

So, the core aspect of Halloween is a remembrance of ancestors and people who have died. What happens in Odisha during Diwali is more similar to it than in the rest of the country.

Lakshmi, the goddess of wealth and prosperity, is worshipped in India during Diwali in most parts of the country, whereas, in Odisha, people pray for their ancestors on this day. To do so, they use *Pimpeii* or *Kaunriya kathi* (that is, jute sticks). On the night of Diwali, families gather around the tulsi or holy basil plant, which is usually planted outside their homes. The rangoli made is in the shape of a boat with seven chambers, each having a special significance. Cotton, salt, mustard, asparagus root, turmeric and a creeper are placed in the outside chambers. The central chamber is kept for prasad (offerings to the gods) and a diya with a jute stick. All the family members light the jute sticks using the central diya. They then raise it to the sky while praying for the departed souls.

> **DAY OF THE DEAD**
>
> Did you know that there is a Mexican equivalent of Halloween celebrated around the same time, with colourful decorations and costumes, when the dead and ancestors are remembered and prayed to? Called Día de Los Muertos (Day of the Dead), one can see altars of the dead ancestors which are built as part of the festival. The latters' favourite dishes are then placed as offerings. A similar ritual in India is Bhoot Chaturdashi observed by Bengalis.

Another legend is connected to Rama's return to Ayodhya and his coronation, a significant event that even the dead wanted to attend! Diyas were lit to give directions to the dead souls to return to earth to witness it.

The Jagannath Temple of Puri is a sacred place where this tradition has been maintained for years. People visit in hordes to pray for their ancestors. There, they stand on the twenty-two steps of the Singhadwara or the Lion Gateway of the temple. They also offer food to the Brahmans. This day is also known as Badabadua Daka or 'summoning ancestors'. On this day, it is believed that forefathers from the other side visit earth to bless their descendants.

However, burning Kaunriya Kathi in huge numbers causes immense air pollution in the temple. Also, the coronavirus pandemic was a cause of concern adding to the fears. This is why this age-old ritual did not happen at the Jagannath Temple of Puri in 2020.

Thus, Odisha's Pimpeii Kathi Daaka too is an important day to remember the dead. Just like Halloween, but without the costumes!

EIGHTEEN

Why Is Diwali Celebrated a Month Later in Himachal Pradesh and Uttarakhand?

Doesn't it feel a little sad when Diwali is over? The electric lights are taken down, the decorations are removed, and life goes back to normal. Well, what if I told you that you could celebrate the festival twice with the gap of a month? All you have to do is visit Himachal Pradesh or Uttarakhand a month after Diwali. In fact, people from these two states living elsewhere usually visit around this time. Here, Diwali is celebrated a month after the entire country. Isn't that surprising? Let us find out why.

Himachal Pradesh and Uttarakhand, as you know, are Indian states with plenty of mountains and hills. Travelling to such places is easier today compared to ancient times. Proper roads have been constructed, making travel faster and smoother. However, this was not the case earlier. There was also no internet, postal or courier service in those times. News had to be physically delivered by a messenger.

When Rama and Lakshmana rescued Sita and returned to Ayodhya, people showed them the path by lighting lamps. Everyone came to know about the end of their exile and their return to the kingdom. However, this news reached the people living in the mountains one month later. And thus, today, many places there observe Diwali a month later as 'Budhi Diwali' or 'Diyai', which is celebrated for five days!

Meanwhile, there are others who say that the people here were busy with farming activities during the main Diwali festival. Budhi Diwali is also significant because it celebrates the death of the snake demons Dano and Asur. Snakes hibernate during the cold months anyway. So, the absence of their sightings during this festival is quite symbolic.

This legend has been passed down from generations, but it is only in the past 200 years that people have been actively observing Budhi Diwali. This is true especially in Shimla, Kullu, and most importantly, Jaunsar-Bawar or Sirmaur, where it is known as Manshaari.

Unlike mainstream Diwali, it is not marked by the loud bangs and bursts of firecrackers. Instead, dhols and nagadas are beaten around bonfires in the middle of the night to kickstart the festival. People burn pine wood, grasses and bunches of Deodar twigs in it. These twigs become nature's phuljaris, so to speak! Women prepare for this festival by planting seeds days before. The sown plant called dibsa is then offered in the bonfire in a flaming torch.

The next day is celebrated with much zest and vigour. People participate in folk dances called Rasa, Badhechu and Budiyat, folk theatre called Swang and traditional sad songs called Virah. The Rasa dance, in which men and women dance in a circle as they sing folk songs, is very popular. Bhand performances of mythological scenes, such as the churning of the ocean (Samudra Manthan), are played out. This is done

---

UNHAPPY DIWALI FOR THARU TRIBE

The Tharu tribe of Kumaon observes Diwali as the day to mourn the dead and pray for their ancestors.

It is said that Rama wanted to dry up the water in the ocean and create a path so that his army could walk across to Lanka and rescue Sita. However, the water god Varuna appeared before him just as he loaded his powerful Brahmastra and promised to help him cross the seas. However, the divine weapon, once loaded, must be discharged. And so, it is believed that Rama directed his Brahmastra towards modern-day Rajasthan and when it fell, it dried up all the water in the region, thus creating the Thar Desert and killing a lot of people (who were the ancestors of the present Tharu people). However, the tribe is now slowly starting to let go of their ancestral worship and rituals and observe mainstream Diwali.

using a ceremonial rope woven out of sabai or bhabur grass, which is first worshipped. It is then used to represent the tug of war between the devas and the asuras.

People enjoy snacks such as Shakuli (Himachali papad) and urad dal pakodas. There's also chiwda or beaten rice and walnuts, which is considered prasad. A pahadi dessert enjoyed in this festival is *Jhangore ki kheer*. While the usual milk, sugar, raisins and cashews are used to make this kheer, the star ingredient is *jhangora* or barnyard millet, instead of rice. And that's how five days of this pahadi eco-friendly Diwali is carried out in these two states. Next time your family plans a holiday, take them to the hills to celebrate Budhi Diwali!

NINETEEN

Why Dogs Are Worshipped by Nepalis

There are two kinds of people in this world. Those who love dogs, and the others who do not know just how lovable and loyal these animals are! It is said that dog is man's best friend. Well, Nepalis certainly are dogs' best friends too because no one loves dogs more than them. They even have an entire festival dedicated to these furry cuties!

That is right. Dogs are worshipped as part of the five-day Diwali or Tihar celebrations. This is not just in Nepal, but also among Nepali communities in India and elsewhere. It is called 'Kukur Tihar' or Khicha Puja by Newars, a group of Nepali people. This day is dedicated to all the domestic and stray dogs. It celebrates the special bond that humans share with these creatures. This is also a day to thank them for their loyalty and friendship. A tika is put on their head along with a garland of flowers around the neck. They are offered various tasty treats, including meat, eggs, milk and dog food.

This celebration among Nepali Hindus during Diwali is not without a reason. There are several legends from our ancient scriptures showing that humans and dogs have been friends for thousands of years. For instance, in the Rig Veda, there is mention of Samara, the mother of dogs. She helps Indra, the lord of the heavens, find stolen cattle.

Another interesting tale finds a mention in the Mahabharata, where it is said that the Pandavas were accompanied by a dog on their way to Swarga or heaven. However, as the journey

HOLY C(R)OW!

Kukur Tihar is only celebrated on the second day of Tihar or Nepali Diwali. On the other days, other creatures are worshipped. The first day is Kaag Tihar, on which they worship crows and ravens, also believed to be messengers of Yama. The third day is celebrated as Gai Tihar, when cows are worshipped. On the fourth day, Calleja, Nepalis worship the ox. It is only on the fifth day that Nepalis celebrate Bhai Tika, cherishing the bond between brothers and sisters.

progresses, four of the five brothers and their wife, Draupadi, lose their way. Yudhishthira is the only one who makes it to heaven accompanied by the dog, without whom he refuses to enter heaven. It is then revealed that the dog was none other than Yama, the god of death.

In fact, dogs are believed to be Yamraj's messenger. He is also said to have two guard dogs—each having four eyes—guarding the gates of hell or Naraka. In fact, this is the reason why this day of Diwali is also called Naraka Chaturdashi. (If you have read or watched the first *Harry Potter*, you will remember Fluffy. He is the three-headed dog guarding the entrance to the Sorcerer's Stone.)

Even in Greek mythology, Hades, the god of the underworld, had a three-headed guard dog called Kerberos. Interesting, is it not? Another god in Hindu mythology who is associated with a dog is Shiva's fiercest manifestation, Bhairava, whose vahana or vehicle was a dog.

Kukur Tihar is no longer a festival celebrated only among Nepalis. Thanks to the internet, people all over the world know about this day that celebrates our four-legged friends. Countries such as Mexico and Australia have also started celebrating this day. In fact, on this day, several dog shelters go the extra mile and celebrate the rescue dogs.

This Diwali might be a great time to celebrate your pet dog. Ask the grown-ups in your family to help you with the tika, the floral garland and some yummy dog treats. And even if you do not have a dog, you can always feed a stray. These loyal creatures will never forget your act of kindness, and you would have made new friends.

※

TWENTY

Why the Cattle Complained to Lord Shiva

The relationship between man and animal dates back to thousands of years. It started right from when cavemen befriended wild dogs for the first time. They helped them hunt for their food. We owe a lot to animals, and therefore several Hindu festivals and temples are centred around celebrating animals or their spirits. After all, India is primarily an agricultural country, where cattle is much revered.

In this chapter, we will focus on the legend behind cattle worship in eastern India. It is said to have begun with the animals calling the divine helpline to complain to Lord Shiva! But why? Let us explore!

It is said that when God created men, he had to provide them with food for a long time. When he grew tired of it, he told mankind to be self-sufficient and grow and get their own food. However, it was quite a task without proper equipment. The humans gave up and confided in Shiva about their problem, who took pity on the mortals and gave them cattle to help with farming. However, there was a condition: that the animals should be treated well. The people readily agreed. And for a while, this arrangement worked out perfectly for everyone. The people harvested food and did not have any scarcity. The cattle, goats and sheep did their work and were treated kindly. However, it was not long before problems started creeping in.

The animals began to realize that they were being overworked. They were not being given good food anymore and their shelters were becoming unhygienic too. Additionally, working longer hours meant they had no time to relax. Now it was their turn to complain to Shiva, who patiently listened to all their woes. He then assured them that he would come

> **ANIMAL WORSHIP**
>
> Hindus worship a wide range of animals, besides domestic ones such as cows and oxen. For instance, did you know that rats have an entire temple dedicated to them? It is the Karni Mata Temple in Bikaner, Rajasthan. Meanwhile, snakes have their own religious festival on the day of Nagpanchami.

to pay a surprise visit and check things for himself. It would be on the no-moon night of the month of Kartik, which is also Diwali.

Luckily for the humans, they came to know of this surprise visit. Fearing the ire of Shiva, they decided to get their act together. They started looking after the cattle and their sheds too. Vermilion was applied on the horns of the animals. The sheds were illuminated with beautiful diyas and quality fodder was provided to the cattle.

If that was not enough, bales of hay were kept outside the sheds and some were stacked on the roofs too. When Shiva finally paid his visit, what he saw made him happy. He found the people praying to Pashupati, the lord of animals. Finding that the problem had been resolved on its own, Shiva left earth.

This became a ritual. It is a day to shower cows and oxen with affection, provide good fodder and clean sheds and worship them. This festival is called Sohrai or Bandna and is mainly celebrated in the east Indian states of Jharkhand, West Bengal, Odisha and Chhattisgarh. The people of the Prajapati, Kurmi, Oraon, Santal and Munda communities celebrate it.

On this day, the women of Hazaribagh, Jharkhand, create beautiful murals on the walls of their mud huts. It is done to observe this special day and it has been in practice since 10,000 BC! Earlier these paintings, which are symbolic of fertility and prosperity, were made on the cave walls. And guess what this art form is called? Sohrai paintings. They are so unique and beautiful that they got the Geographical Indication (GI) tag in 2020. This tag is given to unique products and arts originating in specific places of India.

TWENTY-ONE

Why Diwali Is Special for Newly-Weds in Tamil Nadu

Diwali is a special time of the year for everyone, but it is even more special for newly married couples in Tamil Nadu. Let's read on to find out why.

'Thala' means first or most prominent in Tamil. The 'first' Diwali for newly-weds is most 'prominent'. That is why it is called Thalai Deepavali. The newly married couple visit the girl's house to celebrate this special occasion. They are showered with *seervarisai*, which literally means a line-up of different gifts, including clothes and jewellery, among other things. The origin of this ritual is in the bride's parents wanting to meet their daughter after marriage. They want to ensure that she is being taken care of. The new son-in-law is also showered with expensive gifts such as gold or diamond rings.

Sadly, with time, traditions sometimes tend to get twisted. What was given with generosity and free will earlier, has today become more of a demand by some greedy grooms. For some, it has become the same as dowry.

However, this is not true for all Thalai Deepavali, and most families still celebrate it in its true spirit, which includes a temple visit, seeking blessings from elders and eating plenty of sweets. In fact, the groom's entire family, including parents and siblings, visit the bride's house for this celebration.

Thalai Deepavali celebrations begin before the break of dawn, when the family takes a ritualistic oil bath. After that, the newly-weds accept their new clothes which have been kept at the feet of their deities in the prayer area. This signifies that these gifts have been blessed by the gods.

The bursting of firecrackers begins after this. The family sits together for a

> **ONLY TREATS, NO TUMMY UPSET**
>
> Another interesting and integral part of Deepavali in Tamil Nadu is the ritual of having a medicinal concoction on this day called *lehiyam*, which is a mix of ginger or *inji*, jaggery, cardamom, as well as the seeds of coriander and cumin. Every household has its own style of making this traditional mix, which is consumed in small quantities to ensure healthy digestion during this time of feasting.

lavish breakfast and lunch, but dinner is usually light. It is said that Shiva and Parvati made up after a fight on this day.

Part 5

Other Rituals, Myths and Legends of Diwali

TWENTY-TWO

Why Did Hanuman Swallow the Sun?

What is your absolute favourite character from Hindu mythology? Perhaps Rama, the hero from Ramayana? Or perhaps it is Shiva, the blue-throated god? Maybe Kali, the goddess of time and death? However, Hanuman is one of the most popular characters from Hindu mythology. His legends are replete with magic and wonder. And one of them includes the story of why the monkey-faced deity swallowed the sun. Let's read on.

Remember, when we read earlier about why Hanuman is worshipped on the day of Naraka Chaturdashi? This story offers an alternative reason as to why the second night of Diwali is so dark. And as is common, this story too has several variations and interpretations, with each of them being more interesting than the other. In fact, most of these

> ### STUDENT OF THE YEAR
>
> Young Hanuman once approached Surya, the Sun God, to ask him to be his teacher. However, Surya declined the offer saying he was too busy travelling across the sky all day. So, Hanuman promised to run backwards in front of Surya's chariot across the sky, as this would allow Surya to teach him while being at work. He agreed, and Hanuman, being the son of Vayu, the Wind God, was able to do as he promised. And that is how Hanuman learnt all the Vedas, mantras and verses!

versions do not even mention Hanuman swallowing the sun.

The story goes that once baby Hanuman woke up hungry and could not find either of his parents. He saw the sun and thought it was a ripe, luscious berry and flew straight towards it. As he flew, he kept growing in size till he could swallow the sun. It is said that when he swallowed it, the entire universe was plunged into darkness. In one version, Indra, the lord of the heavens, sent a thunderbolt at the young god, injuring his left chin. He fell and was caught by his celestial father, Vayu, the God of Wind. Such an attack on his son angered Vayu, and he withdrew his breath, which caused the airflow to the universe to stop, thus suffocating all living creatures.

The gods began to panic and along with Brahma, went to Vayu to appease him. Brahma revived the young child and named him Hanuman (meaning 'one with a distinctive chin', due to his permanently disfigured chin). Then, all the gods blessed Hanuman with different boons. Varuna blessed him with fearlessness of water; Surya gave him some of his brightness as well as wisdom; Vishwakarma, the divine architect, gave him immunity from any divine weapon he forges; Brahma too gave him immortality for one cosmic eon; and Vayu blessed his son with the boon that all ghosts and spirits would flee when Hanuman is remembered. Hence, Hanuman is worshipped on the day of Kali Chaudasa, the one day in the Hindu calendar when occult activities abound.

In the second version, Indra does not throw his thunderbolt. Instead, all the gods go to the young one and beg him to release the sun.

There are several other variations of this legend. One of them is how Hanuman spit out the sun after putting it in his mouth. It was not because it hurt him. In truth, the rays of the sun felt like hands, and being a vegetarian, he did not like how it felt inside his mouth. And later when Indra struck him with the thunderbolt, he put it in his mouth as well. He pretended to be injured to maintain Indra's ego.

Another legend talks about how Vayu took his injured infant to Mahakala forest, where he usually worshipped Shiva. Vayu brushed the child's limbs against the Shivalingam while praying to the god. Shiva was pleased and blessed Hanuman with several boons.

There is even an alternate myth which says that Hanuman was not hurt by Indra's thunderbolt and continued to swallow the sun. Ravana came and pulled his tail to stop the giant child, which further enraged him. They battled for a year before Ravana's father came and begged Hanuman to stop.

TWENTY-THREE

The Killing of Hiranyakashipu by Narasimha

What is neither day, nor night? What is neither animal, nor man, nor god? What is neither outside, nor inside? What is neither ground, nor earth?

The answers to these riddles lie in this very exciting story. It is about a powerful king who was killed by a fascinating mythical creature.

In a previous chapter, you already read about how King Bali was sent by Vishnu to the netherworld. In this one, let us explore the story of Bali's great-grandfather Hiranyakashipu, who also met his end at the hands of Vishnu, but in a very different way. This story is very popular in South India during Diwali and its connection to the festival in the rest of India is also very interesting. Settle down because it is a long adventure. Let us explore, shall we?

Let us start at the beginning. Once upon a time, there were two demigod brothers, Jaya and Vijaya, who were the gatekeepers to Vaikuntha, Vishnu's abode. They were also his devout followers. One day, a group of sages known as the Four Kumaras came to see Vishnu. The brothers refused to let them enter, saying that Vishnu was resting. This made the sages furious. They were confident that Vishnu would meet them. As a result, the Kumaras cursed Jaya-Vijaya to be reborn as mere mortals, which caused them to protest loudly.

Vishnu came out to see what the commotion was all about. Jaya-Vijaya begged him to reverse the curse, but this was not possible. Therefore, Vishnu gave them two options instead. They could either be reborn three times on earth as his enemies or seven times as his devotees. The brothers chose the first option as it seemed to be an easier one. They knew that Vishnu would have to visit earth in different avatars to slay them. They would rather meet him in each life as enemies and be killed at his hands than live seven lives without him.

And lo and behold, in their first birth in the Satya Yuga, the siblings were reborn as Hiranyaksha and Hiranyakashipu, but they had no memories of their previous birth. Our story begins when Hiranyaksha had already been killed by Vishnu in his third avatar of Varaha (the boar). This made his younger brother Hiranyakashipu very angry and he hatched an elaborate plan to avenge his brother's death. He performed severed penance to appease Brahma, in the hope that he would grant him a boon—the boon of immortality.

After all, immortality is the most-wanted power in every super villain's bucket list, including Lord Voldemort in *Harry Potter*! However, Brahma could not grant him the boon of immortality as death is inevitable.

Hiranyakashipu decided to lay down a few tough conditions for his death: that he could be killed neither during day nor night, neither inside the house, nor outside; neither by an animal, nor man, nor god; neither on the ground nor the sky.

It is also mentioned in the Mahabharata that Hiranyakashipu performed another penance. This time it was for Shiva. In return, he received unparalleled powers of combat and skill in the use of different weapons. He was also granted superpowers that made him equal to many gods!

With these two boons, Hiranyakashipu became extremely powerful. It is said that he ruled for more than twenty-four Mahayugas, which is more than ten crore years! The only thing he could not earn was the validation of his son, Prahlad, an ardent devotee of Vishnu. For Prahlad, it was Vishnu who was the most powerful. One day, Hiranyakashipu challenged Prahlad. 'Is your Vishnu in that pillar behind you?' he roared, smashing the pillar.

And lo and behold, there appeared from inside the pillar Vishnu in his fourth avatar, Narasimha, part lion and part man. He took Hiranyakashipu and laid him on his thigh. With his claws, the beast tore open his chest, killing him instantaneously.

Wait, if Hiranyakashipu was nearly immortal, how could Narasimha kill him? First, Narasimha was neither whole man,

> **NARASIMHA'S TEMPLE IN PAKISTAN**
>
> After Hiranyakashipu was killed, Prahlad, being Vishnu's devotee, is said to have built a temple for Narasimha at the pillar from which he had appeared. The place was called Mulasthana (or Moolasthana, meaning 'point of origin'). This temple today lies in the region of what we now call Multan, in Pakistan.

nor whole animal, nor whole god: he was a little of all three. Second, it was dusk when he was killed, which means it was neither day nor night. Next, Narasimha killed him on his thigh on the threshold, which is neither inside, nor outside the house. He was neither on ground, nor in the sky. This story proves the inevitability of death.

How is this story related to Diwali? You must be wondering. Well, guess who Jaya-Vijaya were born as in their second mortal life during the Treta Yuga? Ravana and Kumbhakarna! And remember who killed them both? Yes, it was Rama, the seventh avatar of Vishnu. Therefore, the story of Hiranyakashipu's death by Narasimha has a close connection with Diwali. After all, it is the day when Rama returns from Lanka after defeating Ravana. A classic case of history repeating itself!

TWENTY-FOUR

Why Are Cards Played During Diwali?

You are probably too young to know how to play cards, and younger still to play them. While gambling is considered a bad habit in all age groups, grown-ups, for a change, break the rules during Diwali. In case you have never seen this yourself, this happens every year during the festive season, when adults in the family and their friends get together for an evening of playing cards. But why on Diwali?
What is so special about it? Well,
it is not a very difficult mystery to solve.

Cards are played as a ritual after completing Lakshmi Puja, which falls on the third day of Diwali. This is because playing cards is believed to be auspicious during this time. Lakshmi is believed to smile upon the players and wish them luck. However, for someone to win, someone else has to lose, right?

This brings us to the famous game of dice between Shiva and Parvati. Narada, the god-sage who was both a travelling musician and a storyteller, once visited the divine couple in their home on Mount Kailasa and introduced them to this game, which is somewhat similar to Ludo. Parvati had a great time playing the game as she kept winning against her husband.

Thrilled, she declared that anyone who gambles on Diwali night would have great fortune through the whole year. That is the basis for playing the traditional Pachikalu on the fourth night of Diwali. It is played with *dayakattai*, a pair of elongated or cuboid dice, with zero to three dots punched on to each side. These are typically made of brass. The game is played by two or four people. The game of dice has been substituted by the playing of cards. In fact, it is believed that not playing cards on this evening would make you a donkey in your next life.

In fact, it is also believed that Parvati played dice with her sons Ganesh and Kartikeya and the Kailasa Temple in the Ellora Caves of Maharashtra has sculptures of this scene. Thus, it seems gambling

> **DIWALI GAMBLING BEYOND INDIA**
>
> Other than cards, other gambling games too are played during this season. Called Jhandi Munda in India (also known as Langur Burja, Jhanda Burja, Khor Khore and Crown and Anchor), it is hugely popular in Nepal during Tihar.

was a sport that even the gods indulged in. However, Hindu mythology also serves as a caution against the same. In Mahabharata, the five Pandavas lost everything they had in a game of dice, including their wife, Draupadi.

Some believe that the tradition of playing cards started off as part of harvest festival, when famers have money to spend, thanks to their sell of crops. They would celebrate with their friends and family and indulge in a friendly game of dice.

Playing cards, like with every other bad habit, can be harmless and fun if indulged in once a year. After all, with Lakshmi's blessings, you can at least try a hand or two. However, her sister Alakshmi is not far away from those who become addicted to it. They just might end up losing everything, just like the Pandavas.

TWENTY-FIVE

The Real Story of the Importance of Rangoli

Do you know what rangoli is? It is a traditional floor decoration made during important Indian festivals, mostly on Diwali. Even though Holi is the festival of colours, Diwali gets its own splash of colours too, all thanks to beautiful rangoli designs.

But what is the relation of Diwali and rangolis? Isn't this festival all about pretty lights and plenty of food and crackers? We will come to that in the next chapter.

Well yes, but remember the five days of Diwali also include Lakshmi Puja. It is in her worship that rangoli gets it special significance. But first, let us learn a bit more about it.

Did you know rangoli got its name from the joining of two Sanskrit words? 'Rang' means colours and 'avali' means 'row', meaning 'rows of colours'. Rangoli is known by different names in different parts of India. For instance, in my home state Assam, it is called *alpona*. Do you know what it is called in your language?

Traditionally, rangoli was made with natural materials including powdered limestone, coloured sand, flower petals and dry rice flour, designed entirely by hand. However, today designing a rangoli has become easier and more convenient given there are acrylic paints and stencils. The art and tradition of making rangoli is passed down from one generation to the next, but you can always learn from an elder or get a few tips from YouTube videos.

Different states in India have different names and types of rangoli. For instance, in Rajasthan, *mandana* is painted on walls. In Chhattisgarh, *chaook* is drawn in white (dried rice flour or other dust powder) at the entrance of a house. In Maharashtra and Karnataka, rangoli is made on doors of houses to ward off evil. No matter what it is known as, there is a common belief that lines in a rangoli

> **PRETTY YET PRACTICAL**
>
> Do you know that rangolis serve a practical purpose too? The powdered limestone that is used for making rangoli designs prevents insects from entering the house. So, drawing basic designs around the kitchen area is a good way to repel them.

design should not have any unfilled cracks as that allows the entry of evil spirits.

Let us look at how the tradition of making rangoli came into being. One of the stories goes back to when the Pandavas were in exile. Draupadi, their wife, used to draw three lines of rice flour on the hearth before cooking. This was a symbol of gratitude to the sun god, Surya, for giving them the legendary Akshaya Patra, a vessel of plenty that never ran out of food. This is believed to be the humble beginning of rangoli.

However, there are other stories as well. In Tamil Nadu, Andal is worshipped as the only female poet-saint devoted to Lord Vishnu, just like Mirabai. It is said that Andal was so devoted to Vishnu that she married the god. It happened in the Tamil month of Margazhi, which falls around the time of Diwali. It has since given rise to a ritual. During this month, unmarried girls wake up at dawn and make rangoli designs to welcome Lord Vishnu into their homes.

Another origin story begins with the death of a high priest's son. The entire kingdom mourned the death of the priest's son and prayed to Brahma to bring him back to life. Moved by the desperation of the people, Brahma told the king to create the boy's portrait on earth, which he then brought to life. It is believed that this was the first rangoli ever made. Rangolis, since then, have been symbolic of prayers for fulfilment.

As per another myth, one day Narayan, the Supreme Being, made a divine painting of a maiden. He made it with the juice he extracted from a mango tree. Her beauty surpassed that of any creature in heaven and earth. This somehow became an art form for women to express the natural and divine beauty around us.

During Diwali, rangolis are made at the entrance of the house to welcome Lakshmi, the goddess of fortune. Before they are made, the house is cleaned properly to welcome the Goddess, who is believed to visit clean and well-lit homes.

But that is not all. Besides rangolis, it is also a ritual to draw Lakshmi's feet, called *shripada,* pointing inwards. This symbolizes the entry of Lakshmi into the home of her devotees. These auspicious symbols are usually in white, which stand out in the darkness of the evening. Rangoli designs are also drawn on doors and on the lids of coin jars and boxes.

Diwali and Lakshmi Puja are the most radiant of Hindu festivals, all thanks to the intricate and beautiful rangolis that adorn homes and offices. Together, they are festivals of not just light but also happiness and prosperity.

TWENTY-SIX

Are Fireworks Really a Part of Diwali?

What do you like the most about Diwali? Is it the beautiful earthen diyas and electric lights? Or the colourful rangolis? Maybe the yummy sweets and delicacies? Or is it the crackers and fireworks? If it is the last one, you are going to enjoy reading this chapter.

What if I told you that firecrackers were never part of Diwali? Pretty shocking, right?

Over 2,000 years ago, when Diwali was first celebrated, it was a simple affair. People only used to clean and decorate their homes and light earthen diyas outside. Besides, they banged pots and pans to ward off misfortune (remember this for later). At most they would light incense sticks, light bonfires and play the dhol.

There were no sparklers or crackers such as rockets,

parachutes and flowerpots. Why? Fireworks had still not come to India. Isn't that surprising? It used to be a quiet and peaceful Diwali in the olden days. Some ancient texts reveal that saltpetre was probably used in India over a thousand years ago. It is an ingredient in gunpowder, which is in turn used to make firecrackers. But festive firecrackers were still hundreds of years away from being used in the celebration of Diwali.

Do you know where these crackers really came from? China! In fact, gunpowder is one of the Four Great Inventions that the Chinese boasts of (the other three being the compass, papermaking and printing). The first use of gunpowder in firecrackers was in the seventh century during the Tang Dynasty. They believed that the loud bursts of sounds and sparks of light would chase off any negative energy or spirits around them. They were not very different from their Indian brothers and sisters after all, right?

Now, regional specialities or things that belong to a particular place do not necessarily stay put there, but can be transported to and replicated in other places as well. For instance, dosa might be a South Indian speciality, but it is found everywhere in India and the world. Similarly, most historians believe that gunpowder too came to India via Arab traders. It started being used in weapons and fireworks after AD 1400. So, it was more than 700 years after its first use in China. So, even if ancient texts mention saltpetre, it was not really in use. That is, until Arab traders brought the gunpowder technology from China to India and even Europe.

> **DANGER IN THE AIR**
>
> Did you know that thirty-five Indian cities find their names listed among 'the world's 50 most polluted cities in 2020', which means that 70 per cent of the cities are in India? Ask a grown-up to check if your city is among those.

How do we know that? Well, there is no mention of the use of fireworks in Diwali before the fifteenth century. One of the earliest mention of fireworks in India was in a sixteenth-century Sanskrit text called *Kautukachintamani*. It lists out the ingredients required to make fireworks as sulphur, charcoal, saltpetre, quicksilver, bamboo hollows and even cow urine! Foreigners who visited India do mention firework displays; however, those were only witnessed in weddings and festivals and that too only after 1500.

Although fireworks came in use around 500–600 years ago, not every household bought *phuljaris* and *anars* during Diwali, as they were very expensive. Only the royal families, nobles and the rich could afford to buy fireworks on festive occasions.

In fact, it was a sign of wealth and status to have firework displays. During the Mughal rule, they became increasingly popular during coronations, weddings and festivals. Even then, firecrackers during Diwali probably started sometime after the eighteenth century. Then, Maratha kings started organizing firework displays for the public.

It took over a century for the first fireworks factories to

start production for the public. The first factories started in Kolkata and more famously, Sivakasi, which is known as the fireworks capital of India.

Today, we cannot imagine Diwali without crackers. This is despite the fact that every year many children injure themselves while playing with them. Well, traditions change and evolve. There was no Christmas tree in the first Christmas celebrations, but now it is an essential part of the festival.

However, earlier firecrackers did not cause the problems they do now. In fact, earlier, one could even support it scientifically. The smoke and dangerous gases produced by crackers helped get rid of insects such as mosquitoes and flies. However, they are now available in plenty everywhere for cheap. India already has such a big population. So, now it creates a lot of air, sound and land pollution. This causes immense harm to the elderly, young children, sick people, and even animals and birds. Do you know that air pollution is the second-deadliest killer in India? Sad, but true.

With the growing threat to the environment, we need to look at alternative ways to celebrate Diwali. After all, Diwali is the festival of lights, not sound, right?

TWENTY-SEVEN

Why Are Owls Killed During Diwali?

In India, calling someone an 'ullu' or an owl means that they are stupid. But in truth, owls are considered one of the wisest birds, not just in our country, but in others as well. So if you are called an ullu, be proud. You are certainly smarter than the other person.

In India and especially in Hinduism, sighting of an owl is believed to be ominous as well as auspicious. Owls, or the White Barn Owl, to be specific, are associated with the Goddess of fortune and wisdom, Lakshmi. In Bengali households, one never chases away a White Barn Owl. But then, other types of owls are supposedly a sign of evil.

Lakshmi is believed to visit our homes during Diwali, but she is sometimes accompanied by her elder sister, Alakshmi, the goddess of misfortune. And can you guess which creature is associated with her? If you said owl, you are correct.

On the one hand, owls are considered a symbol of fortune. They are very smart, very fast and can hunt their food even in complete darkness. And you can only bring Lakshmi or good fortune to your house if you yourself are smart and fast like an owl. On the other hand, people are also scared of owls because these birds are associated with the dark or night.

So, you see, people are confused whether owls are actually good or bad omens. And so, they have come up with different superstitions to help them decide when it is good and when it is bad.

If someone hears an owl hooting when they are travelling, it is believed to be a good sign. But if an owl comes to their house again and again, it is said to be bad. If you see or hear it on your left, it is good. But if they are seen or heard from your right, it is bad.

Good or bad, in India, they are treated very poorly during Diwali. How? People who believe in black magic or tantriks, hold the view that sacrificing an owl during Diwali can trap Lakshmi. She can be forced to stay in their house. These people also believe that each part of the owl, right from its ears to its talons, has magical and medicinal properties. Tantriks and

> **CLASS-IFYING OWLS**
>
> Did you know that owls and swans are considered high-class birds, as opposed to low-class birds such as crows and vultures? Well, high-class or not, it is certainly illegal to kill owls, just like tigers or rhinos.

other foolish people believe that Diwali night is the most powerful night to make such magic work. Isn't that funny? Well, it seems grown-ups also believe in their own fairy tales! At least Harry Potter teaches children to be good, kind and brave, with or without magic. Speaking of Harry Potter, do you know that his friendly and loyal pet is a snowy owl, Hedwig?

India is home to around thirty species of owls, and fifteen of them are in danger of being captured, sold or killed during the festive season. Some of the most traded owl species include Mottled Wood-Owl, Brown Fish Owl, Dusky Eagle-Owl, Indian (rock) Eagle Owl and Indian Scops Owl.

This Diwali, let us celebrate the festival of lights and happiness more responsibly, without harming the environment and definitely not owls. They are harmless birds, hunting rodents only for food. Also, did you know that owls mate for life? Once they find a partner, they are so loyal that they never seek another. This is true even if their partner is not there anymore. Now isn't that sweet? All the more reason to treat them with kindness.

Acknowledgements

My first note of gratitude is to my lovely daughter, Zoe. She is the eternal inspiration and source of motivation for all my endeavours. I would also like to thank my parents, Moni Saikia and Jyoti Changmai Saikia, for always encouraging me. I am grateful to my husband Dibyendu Deb Roy for pushing me ahead to thrive in everything I am passionate about.

This work is a fruit of labour gently nurtured by the constant support of my personal legion of goddesses, my friends Swatie, Rohini Deb, Rashee Mehra, Sahiba Sethi, Pallabi Baruah, Pratiksha Patwari, Sunayana Baruah, Satabdee Borah, Trishna Das, Sushmita Mazumdar, Richa Devi and Sangita Kalita.

This book took me on a figurative journey across the country and beyond in search of legends. In this trip, I cannot but thank Venkatesh P.P., Ashwini Motwani and Sayali Barathe for their invaluable contribution.

Made in the USA
Monee, IL
03 May 2026